The Yellow Book of wordplay Stories

Written and Illustrated by

Susan Batko

Vocab Incorporated • Chicago

Consultant: Ruth Hoffmeyer, M.A.

Designer: Carol Becker

Cover Photographer: Daniel Czubak

Home Distributor:
The Southwestern Company
Franklin, Tenn. 37064

National School and Library Distributor:
Communacad
Wilton, Conn. 06897

Printed in the United States of America

Library of Congress Catalog Card Number: 77-70443

ISBN 0-918468-01-9

2 3 4 5 6 7 8 9 10 11 12 13 14 15 BA 86 85 84 83 82 81 80 79 78 77

Contents

The Ghost Who Loved Toast

There once was a ghost
Who ate nothing but toast.
He spread it with butter and honey.

4

spread

5

He dreamed of the taste
As he patted his waist.
And for bread he spent all of his money.

7

His mother was sad.
And his father was mad.
"You are getting too heavy!" they said.

heavy

8

light

"A ghost must be light
To fly through the night.
You really must stop eating bread!"

9

"Tomorrow I'll eat
Just a carrot and beet,"
He promised his father and mother.

10

promised

"But for dinner tonight,
I must have a bite
Of toast with some honey and butter!"

Hi, I'm Kathy!

Hi! My name is Kathy.
Today lots of things went wrong.
But in the end, most of them
came out all right.

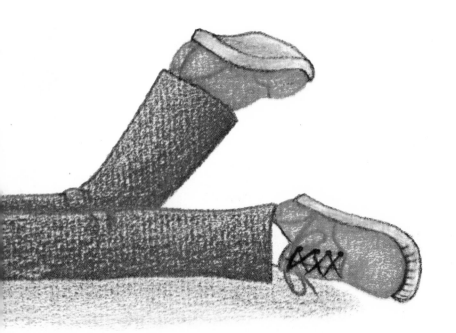

This morning my friend got
mad at me for nothing at all.
And she acted like my enemy.
"Kathy, I don't want to play with
you any more!" she screamed.

enemy

But later she told me that she was sorry.
And we got together again.

together

This afternoon my sister found
me on her bed playing with the dog.
"Kathy, there's dog hair all
over my blanket!" she yelled.
Oh, she was angry!

angry

But later she hugged me.
And she was very gentle.

gentle

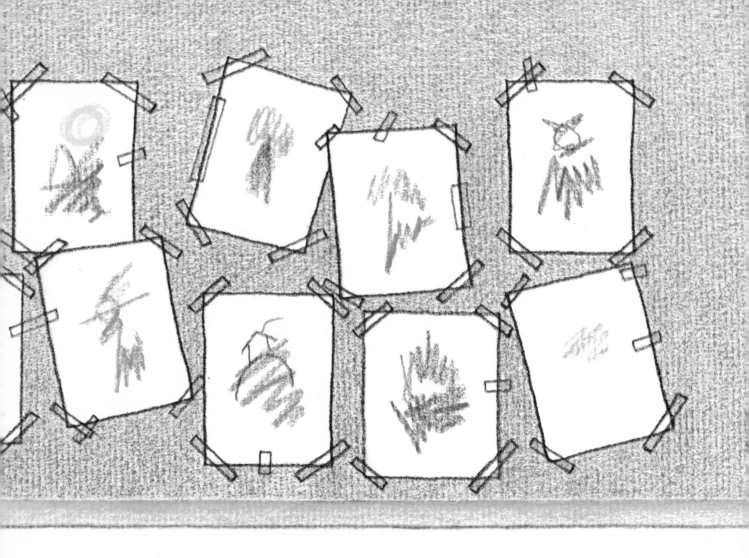

Then my little cousin came over.
"Gee, Kathy, you have lots of new
crayons, paper, and tape!" she said.
And in no time, she wasted all of them.

wasted

But before she went home,
she gave me two big marbles.
She knows that I save them.

save

After dinner I ran outside to
play baseball.
My friends shouted, "Come on, Kathy!
Hit the ball just once!"
Even though I tried as hard as I
could, I failed.

failed

But sooner or later,
I know I'm going to succeed.
I never give up!

succeed

Miss Chimp's Painting Team

entered

One day Miss Chimp entered her
classroom carrying a big bag.
It was filled with paint brushes and
jars of red, blue, and yellow paint.

"What are we going to do?" asked Alice.

Miss Chimp said, "We are going to
cover a wall with newspaper and
paint a big picture."

The class jumped up and down and
acted like monkeys.

Miss Chimp told them to be
quiet and gave each one a job.
"Billy, get the tape from
my desk," she said.

lower

"Wendy, get the newspaper
from the lower shelf of the bookcase.
Alice, help Wendy and Billy tape the
newspaper to the wall."

"Billy won't let me use
the tape!" said Alice.

Miss Chimp said, "Don't waste time.
Take turns using the tape."

"What can I do?" asked Fred.

"You can help me with the paint,"
said Miss Chimp.
She put some blue and some yellow paint
into a dish.
Then she told Fred to mix them.

"They turned green!" said Fred.

mix

Miss Chimp smiled.
She told Fred to measure a cup of
red paint and put it into a dish.
Then she told him to measure a cup of
yellow paint and mix it with
the red paint.

measure

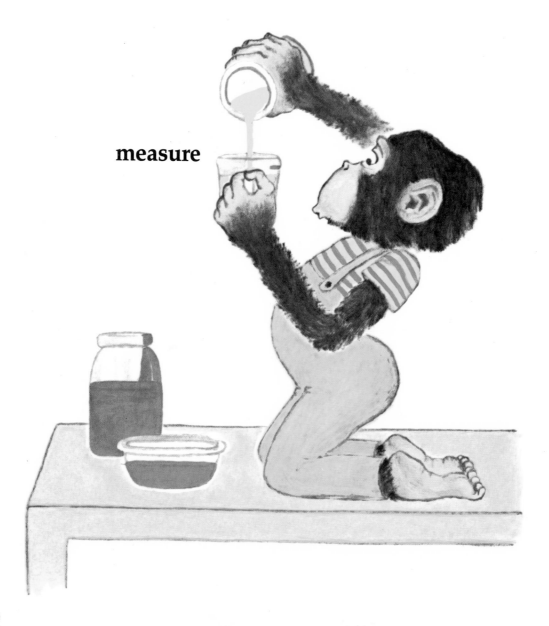

"Look! Now I have orange!" said Fred.
He held up the paint dish for
everyone to see.

"Make some purple!" Wendy yelled.
"That's the color I like!"

"I like blue!" called Alice.

"I like green!" shouted Billy.

45

Soon Wendy, Billy, and Alice
had put up most of the newspaper.

"Do we need more?" asked Billy.

Alice picked up the last piece of
newspaper and said, "No. This is
just enough to cover the wall."

enough

47

Fred was still mixing colors.
"Hey, look!" he called out.
"Red and blue make purple!"

The other chimps ran over to the
paint table.
"Mix all of the colors together," said Wendy.

Fred put some red, blue, and
yellow paint into a dish.
Then he mixed them.

"That looks like mud," said Alice.

"That's not mud," said Fred.
"That's brown, and I like it!"

Miss Chimp said, "Hurry up, now!
Put on your paint clothes, and
start to paint!"

Billy was ready first.
He put some green paint
in the center of the newspaper.

"That looks like the nose of
a witch!" said Wendy.

All of the chimps laughed.

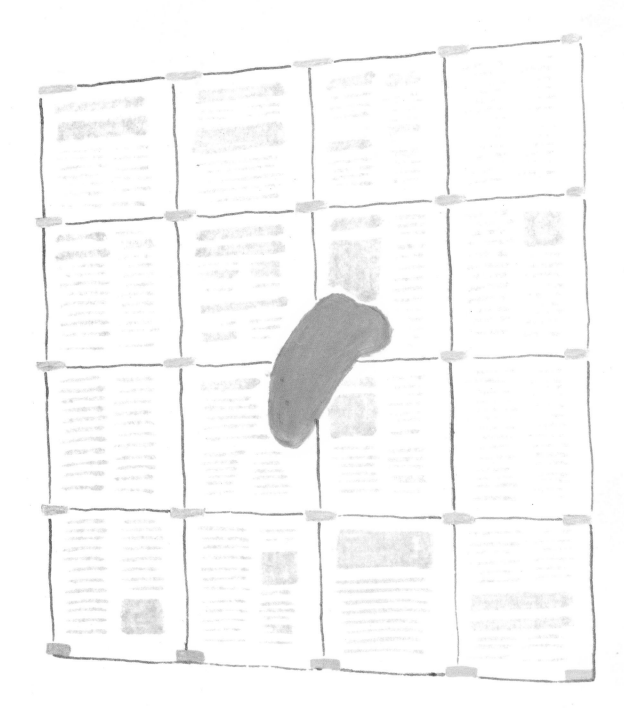

center

Then they began to paint other shapes on
the newspaper.

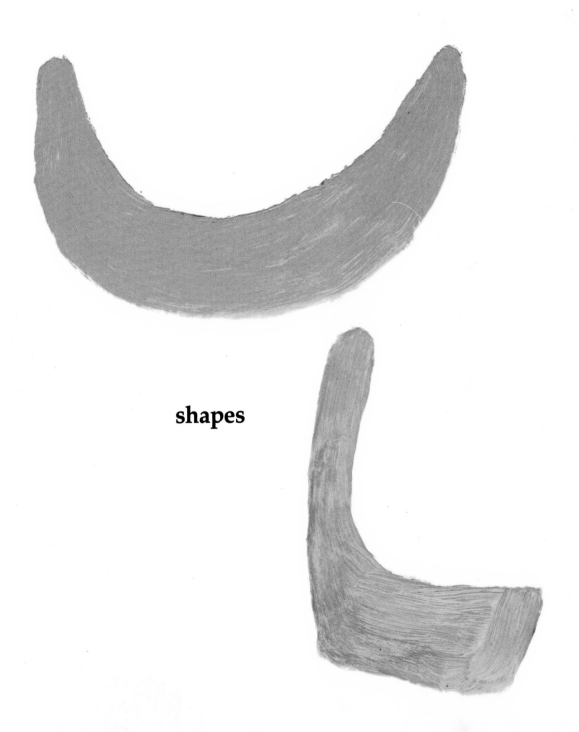

shapes

53

"Let's all paint the same shape in the same color!" said Wendy.

So they all painted big red circles.

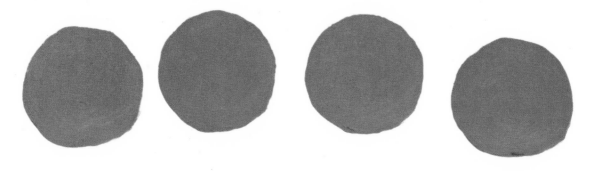

same

"Now let's each paint a different
shape in a different color!" said Billy.

So they painted different shapes in
yellow, blue, orange, and green.

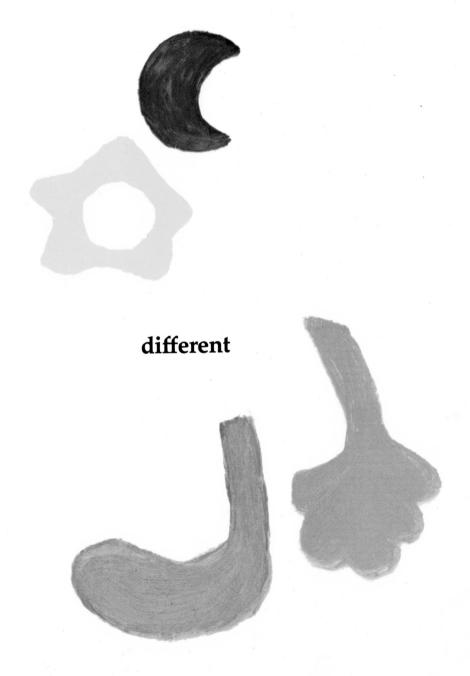

different

Miss Chimp played a happy song on
the piano to help them swing their brushes.

But Alice did not look happy.
"Stop trying to paint my part of
the picture!" she said to Billy.

"It's not your part of the
picture," Billy said.
"No one gave it to you!"

part

59

upper

60

Miss Chimp put Billy on a ladder.
"You help Wendy paint the upper
part of the picture," she said.

After that the room became very quiet.
All of the painters were working hard.

It was not long before they were done.

Miss Chimp told them to step back so they could see the whole picture.

"Wow! It's beautiful!" said Billy. "How did we ever do it?"

"Teamwork!" said Miss Chimp.

whole

The Muddiest Pig Contest

It was the first day of May.
Every year on that day, the pigs in
Mudtown set up the fair at
the Mudtown park.
Many of them were already hard at work.
Susan Pig put on her old blue dress and
ran to help.

among

At the park, the mayor stood on
a box among the workers and told
them what to do.

He called out directions to everyone.
"Put the horses on the merry-go-round!
Put the seats on the ferris wheel!
And put up the tents for the food!"

directions

Then the mayor called Susan and
some of her friends together.
He explained how to set up
the contests and games.

explained

practiced

The pigs had lots of fun while they
were setting up the fair.
They talked about all of the pies they
were going to eat in the
pie-eating contest.
They practiced their grunts and
squeals for the grunting and
squealing contest.
And they laughed when they thought about
getting muddy in the muddiest pig contest.
That was the contest that every pig
in town wanted to win most of all.

When their work was done,
the pigs began to leave the park.
Susan stopped to look at
the statue of Morris Pig—
The Muddiest Pig of All Time.
It was the most important
statue in Mudtown.

important

MORRIS PIG

72

Morris had won the muddiest
pig contest over a hundred years ago.
Since then many other pigs had
won this contest.
But none of them had been
as muddy as Morris.
That is why he was called
The Muddiest Pig of All Time.

"This year I am going to win the
contest," Susan said to the statue.
"And I am going to be even
muddier than you were!"

The next day, the fair opened.
The pigs rode on the merry-go-round and
the ferris wheel.
They ate thousands of hot dogs and
french fries.
They drank hundreds of barrels of root beer.
And they played every game at the fair.

Then it was time for the contests.
The pie-eating contest was first.
Harold Hog said that he could eat
100 raisin-prune pies.

"That's not possible," thought Susan.

But it was possible.
Harold ate every one of them.
He was too full to get up from
the table.
It took four pigs to carry
Harold away.

possible

The grunting and squealing contest
was next.
Rosie Pig was so loud that everyone
else soon gave up.
Rosie had won,
but she kept on grunting and squealing.

Susan and the other pigs had to press
their feet against their ears to keep
out the noise.
Rosie would not stop until the mayor
pinned the blue ribbon on her.

press

At last it was time for the
muddiest pig contest!
All of the pigs lined up to take showers.
Every one of them hated to use
soap and water.
But every one of them had to do it.

discovered

If one little bit of dirt was
discovered on a pig's body,
that pig could not enter the contest.

After their showers, the pigs
were given pails of water.
The mayor said, "All of you know
what to do!
When I blow my whistle, start to
make your mud puddles!"
The pigs squealed and raised
their pails.

raised

At the sound of the whistle,
the pigs went wild.
Most of them just threw their
water on the ground and
rolled around in it.
They were more wet than muddy.

wild

A few pigs took the time to make
mud puddles and take mud baths.
They were really muddy!

few

But what about Susan Pig?
There was only a big mud hole where
she had been standing.
Her friends looked all around.
No one could find her.

Then the mud in the mud hole made
a sudden move.
First it sat up.

sudden

Then it stood up.

88

Then it raised its arms and smiled!

"What is that?" cried the mayor,
pointing at the mud.

The mud said, "It is I, Susan Pig!"

"Susan, is that you?" asked the mayor.
The other pigs squealed and
clapped their feet.
Susan had won the contest.
Her smile became bigger as
the mayor gave her the blue ribbon.

Suddenly the crowd
stopped squealing and clapping.

They looked closely at Susan.

They looked closely at the statue of
Morris Pig.

Then they looked back at Susan.
"Hurray!" they shouted.
"Susan Pig is even muddier than Morris!
Susan Pig is The Muddiest Pig of All Time!"

Don Pedro
and the Three Dragons

Long ago many young knights
lived in a castle in Spain.

An old knight named Don Pedro
also lived there.

Things were quiet until—

three dragons moved into a
cave near the castle.

Because they were dragons,
they liked to roar and blow fire.
They also liked to destroy stone walls with
their heavy tails.
Before long, things weren't quiet any more.

destroy

The young knights knew what
had to be done.
Early one morning, they got on
their horses and set out to
catch the dragons.

"Wait for me!" shouted Don Pedro.
"I'll show those dragons a thing or two!"

But the young knights refused to
let Don Pedro go with them.
"This is no job for an old man,"
said one of them.

refused

remain

"Besides, someone must remain at
the castle," said another knight.
"There's a lot of
work to do around here!"

Don Pedro was angry.
He kicked open the
castle door and went inside.

The young knights rode off toward
the dragons' cave.
The knights thought the dragons
would still be sleeping.
But the dragons were up early too.
They saw the knights coming and
had time to escape.

escape

While the knights looked inside the cave, the dragons ran straight to the castle! They knew it was the last place the knights would look for them.

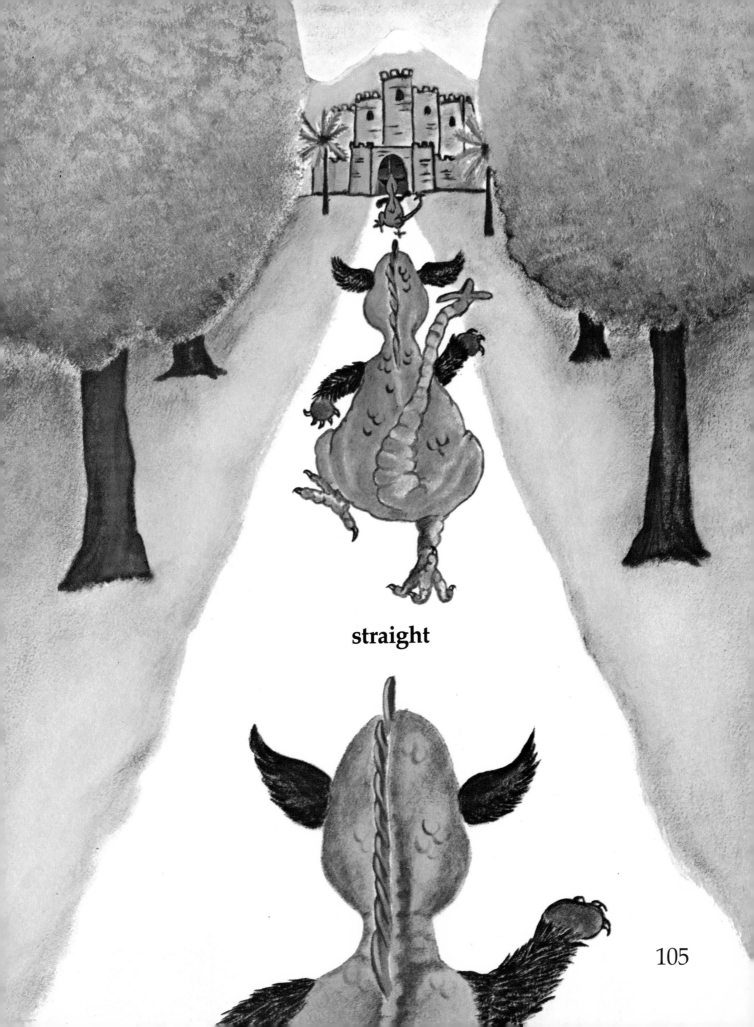

straight

At the castle, Don Pedro was going
about his duties.
He had already washed the bed sheets and
hung them out to dry.
Now he was making a pot of soup.
Suddenly he heard loud noises outside.

✓wash
cook
clean

duties

107

He opened the kitchen door.
There were the three dragons!
When they saw the old knight,
they all laughed.
Don Pedro closed the door quickly.
He laughed too.
"Three dragons all to myself," he thought.

The dragons had already begun
to pound the castle wall with their tails.
There was no time for Don Pedro to get
his sword and shield.

pound

So he picked up the biggest
bread board and pot cover in the
kitchen and ran outside.
By that time, the dragons had made
a big hole in the wall.

When he saw the hole, Don Pedro
shouted, "That does it!
Now you dragons are really going
to get it!"
Then he started after
them swinging his bread board.

The dragons laughed out loud.
They roared and blew fire into
his pot cover.
Then they began to skip around the castle.
They were sure that Don Pedro was
too old and too slow to catch them.

But Don Pedro could run faster than
the dragons thought he could.
Soon he was close enough
to strike their tails.
He hit them hard with his bread board.

strike

The dragons stopped skipping and
turned around.
They weren't laughing any more.
Don Pedro turned around too, and he
ran the other way.
The dragons ran after him.
That was just what Don Pedro
wanted them to do.

He knew what was around the next
corner of the castle.
"Can't catch me!" he shouted as
he turned the corner.
The dragons ran faster.

When they turned the corner, there
was a clothesline full of sheets right
in front of them!
The dragons were going too fast to stop.
They ran into the clothesline and
were caught in the sheets.
Don Pedro laughed as he
watched them try to get free.
The dragons pushed and kicked and
swung their tails.
They turned this way and
that way and that way and this way.

Soon the dragons had rolled themselves and
the sheets into one great big ball.
Quickly Don Pedro tied the
clothesline around them.
Just to make sure they couldn't escape,
he used his bread board to guard them.

guard

Finally the young knights came back to
the castle.
And were they surprised!
There were the three dragons tied
up in sheets.
And there was Don Pedro guarding
them with a bread board.

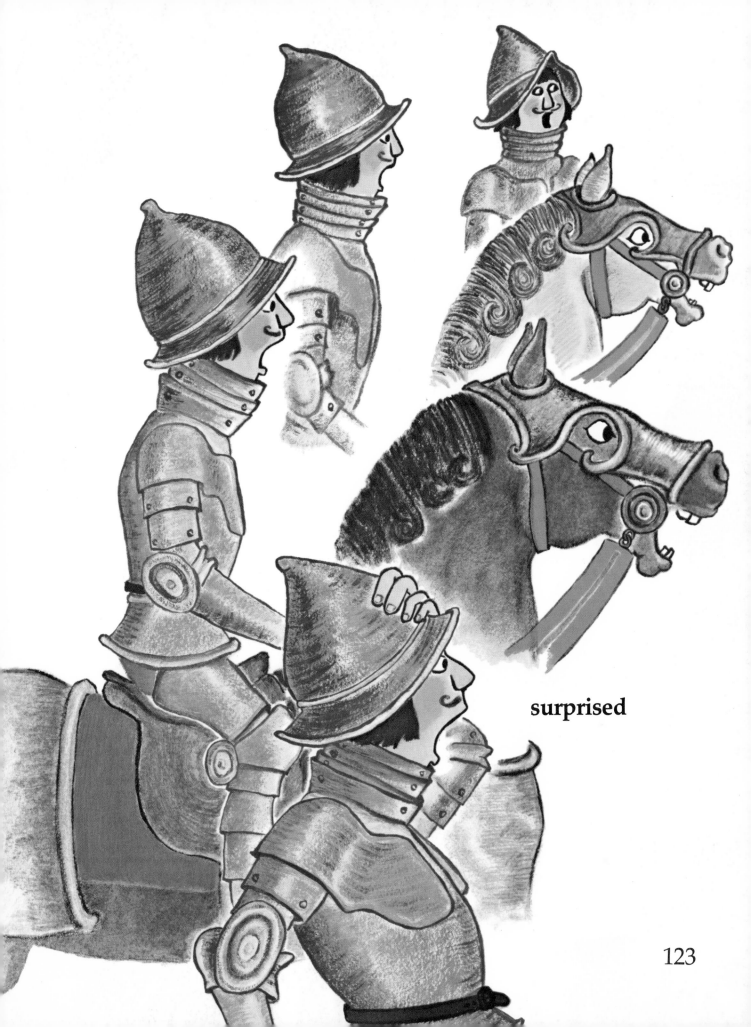

surprised

123

When Don Pedro told the knights about
the hole in the wall, they were very angry.
They jumped off their horses,
pulled out their swords, and cut the
sheets away from the dragons.
The dragons knew they were in danger.

danger

"Get up and start putting that wall
back together!" the knights shouted.
The dragons knew they had to obey.

obey

Late that night, the dragons
were still working on the wall.
The knights were having a party in
the castle.
Don Pedro had been given the seat of
honor at the dinner table.

honor

"Tell us again how you caught the three dragons!" shouted the young knights.

Don Pedro waved his bread board in the air and told the whole story one more time.